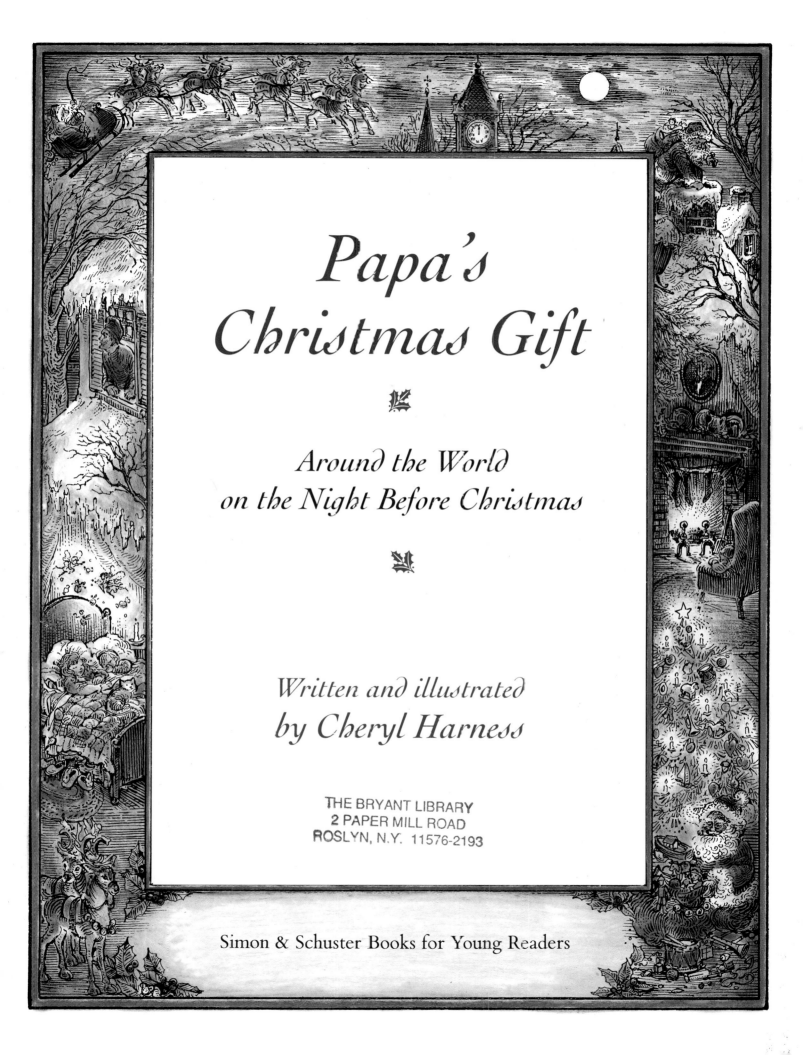

Papa's Christmas Gift

*Around the World
on the Night Before Christmas*

*Written and illustrated
by Cheryl Harness*

Simon & Schuster Books for Young Readers

SIMON & SCHUSTER BOOKS FOR YOUNG READERS
An imprint of Simon & Schuster Children's Publishing Division
1230 Avenue of the Americas, New York, New York 10020

SIMON & SCHUSTER BOOKS FOR YOUNG READERS is a trademark of Simon & Schuster.

Book design by Cathy Bobak.
The text for this book is set in Bembo.
The illustrations are rendered in pen and ink and colored pencil.
Manufactured in the United States of America
First edition
10   9   8   7   6   5   4   3   2   1

Library of Congress Cataloging-in-Publication Data
Harness, Cheryl.
Papa's Christmas gift / written and illustrated by Cheryl Harness.
— 1st ed.
p.   cm.
Summary: Depicts happenings in countries around the world on
Christmas Eve, 1822, while Clement Clarke Moore gives to his family
the first reading ever of his poem "A Visit from Saint Nicholas."
ISBN 0-689-80344-3
1. Christmas—Juvenile poetry.   2. Children's poetry, American.
[1. Christmas—19th century—Poetry.   2. Moore, Clement Clarke,
1779–1863—Poetry.   3. American poetry.]   I. Title.
PS3558.A624762P37   1995
811'.54—dc20   95-2579

To my family

Chelsea House

HOME OF THE MOORE FAMILY

Author's Note

When Clement Clarke Moore was born in New York City in 1779, soldiers were fighting the Revolutionary War. He grew up to be a professor of Asian and Greek literature. Dr. Moore wrote his famous poem for his wife, Catharine, and their six children: Margaret, Charity, Benjamin, Mary, Clement, and the new baby, Emily.

At the time the poem was born, a mighty ditch was being dug from Lake Erie to the Hudson River. It would become the amazing Erie Canal. The great and fierce Napoléon, whose empire nearly covered Europe, had died in the spring of 1821.

The people of Greece were fighting to be independent of the Ottoman Turks. Simón Bolívar was leading the peoples of South America against the Spaniards in battles for freedom. He was known as El Libertador (The Liberator). In Africa, Shaka the Great had formed the Zulu Empire.

James Monroe was the president in Washington, D.C., and in Boston the streets were bright with gaslight for the first time.

This was the world of Christmas Eve 1822, when Clement Moore read to his family his gift to them—and to us: *A Visit from Saint Nicholas*.

" 'Tis Christmas Eve," said Professor Moore.
"Our stockings are hung;
  the wreath's on the door."
Mama lit the candles shining on the tree.
Papa said, "Children, gather now.
  Come, sit by me!
My dears, I've written a poem to share...."

He rustled his papers, settled deep in his chair.

" 'Twas the night before Christmas," Papa read.

Visions of Santa danced in their heads.

By the flickering fire, the children listen
    with delight

As high above the great round world,
    a sleigh flies through the night.

Reindeer fly through the dark sky over the roofs
With moonlight on sleigh bells, antlers, and hoofs.
Over housetops and forests off to the west,
Trappers camp by the river; mules stand at rest.
Icy winds blow. Fire flickers low.
Out in the wilderness. Out in the snow.

Down the dark river to the broad plantations
Southern kitchens are a 'buzz
   with Christmas preparations.
Mists curl through pine and live oak trees,
'Round homes big and small, slave and free.
Songs are sung for the Christ Child's borning
And freedom coming, some glad morning.

Nine nights of Posada lead up to Christmas Day.
Through the streets and piazzas, people make their way
To a house where children ask, "May we have a place to stay?"

It is the Bethlehem story they play
of Mary and Joseph long ago—
except that this is Mexico.

There's feasting to follow,
games and singing!
Hit the piñata bouncing, swinging.

Faster than eagles the reindeer fly, over the salty seas,
Over islands and laughing mermaids, over beaches, palmy trees,
Over pirate ships and fishing boats, tall ships with flags and sails.
Speed away, magic sleigh, high over the spouting whales.

In the Land of the Rising Sun
A winter morning has begun.
Temple bells ring in the day:
Westerners are far away.

Howls of wind and wolves echo from afar,
Across the Russian plains and mountains,
The white lands of the czar.
Southward lies Mongolia and China the
    imperious,
Then Tibet, Siam, and Burma, and India,
    mysterious.

In African treetops green and tall,
Monkeys chatter; bright birds call.
Lions chase zebras through the grassland
As the Nile winds through a sea of sand.
The time of harvesting has come:
Give thanks in dance! Sound the drum!

Bedouins ride on camels tall;
On dunes and tents their shadows fall.
Sway away, rock away, plod away all.

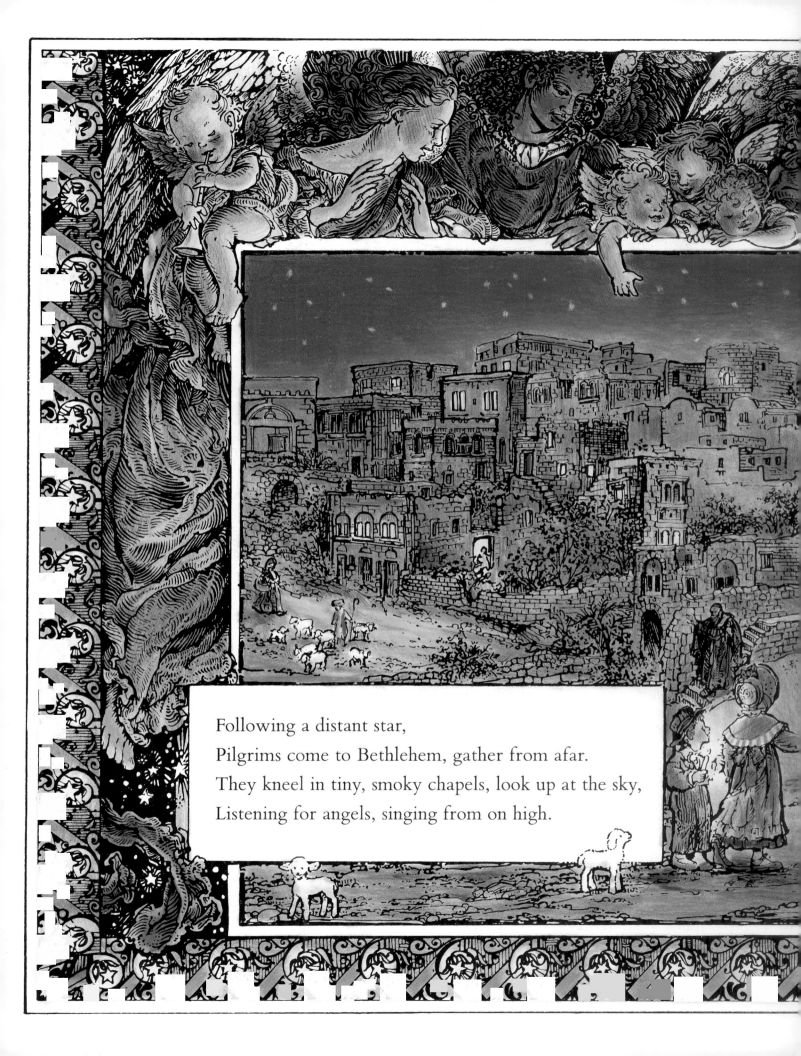

Following a distant star,
Pilgrims come to Bethlehem, gather from afar.
They kneel in tiny, smoky chapels, look up at the sky,
Listening for angels, singing from on high.

While his family listens to Papa spin his Christmas rhyme,
Far across the ocean, at that very time,
Choirs carol *Stille Nacht* in Vienna; stained windows shine red.
Herr Beethoven walks in drifting snow, hearing music in his head.

Jacob and Wilhelm, the two Grimm brothers,
Sit by the fire telling tales told by others:
Tales of princes and maidens and wicked
stepmothers.

Before dawn Dutchmen go out in the cold
To greet Christmas Day with songs of old.
Their carols rise up to the sky,
The moon and stars are glistening.
Children are nestled all snug in their beds
under the blankets, listening.

Torches on gondolas throw gleams and sparks
On the dark canals of Venice
   on the way to Saint Mark's,
The cathedral with bell towers and golden domes
Where pigeons make their lofty homes.

Wearing a crown and golden pants,
A new Louis sits on the throne of France.
He eats Christmas dinner with the noble
    and the knighted.
Napoléon's dead. He's not invited.

Alighting from a crowded sleigh or from a coach-and-four,
English merrymakers gather, throw wide the manor door.
Yule log crackles, sleigh bells jingle-jing.

"Carve the roast! Cut the pies!

Let us have a sing!

Pass the nog and pour the punch!

What will Father Christmas bring?"

Papa took a bow when he read the final line,
And blushed. "If my students heard this poem of mine,
They'd think me quite ridiculous."

"Papa," cried the children, "let's stay up to see Saint Nicholas!"
"Mercy!" said their mother. "With those reindeer and that sleigh,
I could spin about the world and be back on Christmas Day!"

The family climbed the stairs by candlelight.
"Sweet dreams! Say your prayers. Sleep tight!

Happy Christmas to all and to all a good night!"